ALL THESE THINGS

ALL THESE THINGS

A Love Story of Mary and Joseph

Harriet Oxford Kidd

To Evelyn Kidd
Love
Harriet O. Kidd
April 12, 1998

VANTAGE PRESS
New York

All biblical quotations were taken from the Revised Standard Version (1952) of the scripture.

Illustrated by Rosanne Kaloustian

FIRST EDITION

Published by Vantage Press, Inc.
516 West 34th Street, New York, New York 10001

Manufactured in the United States of America
ISBN: 0-533-12272-4

Library of Congress Catalog Card No.: 97-90043

0 9 8 7 6 5 4 3 2 1

To my sister, Jacqueline Johnston Gay

ALL THESE THINGS

I

Anna's fingers were deft and quick as she kneaded the bread her family would eat for their evening meal. Her thoughts, however, were not on the bread, but on the slender girl who sat quietly in the doorway of the small room used for the cooking, eating, and social life of the Hebrew family. The sun was warm in the small courtyard, and the girl seemed lost in a dream.

She has never been like other maidens, the woman thought. *Always quiet, gentle, and kind, but with the look of a dreamer in the dark intelligent eyes. She looks as though she waits for something to happen, patiently but expectantly. Yet,* Anna's thoughts went on, *she seems content and happy. She is quite willing to marry Joseph, in fact*—Anna smiled a little—*she is getting a little impatient with her father in this matter of her wedding.*

The girl, as though her mother had spoken aloud to her, turned and asked, "Mother, do you think I shall make Joseph a good wife?"

Anna, startled for a moment, answered, "I think you will make a most excellent wife, my child. You must learn, however, to be a little less the dreamer. Remember, a husband is master of his household. He expects from his wife all her attention to his needs. You could perhaps be a little more practical," she gently chided. "But I'm sure when you have a home of your own with your Joseph, all will be well with both of you. You are well trained in your duties, both as a wife and as a Hebrew woman. You will be a credit to the House of David," and Anna spoke with great pride as she uttered these last words.

"You have been a wonderful teacher, my mother," the girl

1

said softly, "and I shall do all I can to make Joseph a good wife. Has my father set our wedding day as yet?"

"No," the woman stated, with a shake of her head, "but I think perhaps he will do so very quickly now. The proper time has been awaited since your betrothal, and you know he will abide by the law in all things pertaining to these matters."

"Joseph is a very kind man, is he not, Mother?" Mary asked, then as if an afterthought, "and he is quite handsome, is he not?"

Anna laughed aloud. "You have known Joseph all your life, Mary. He is your kinsman, from the House of David, as you are. He loves you devotedly and has been like a son to your father, since the death of his own father, Jacob, when he was a child. Yes, I think your father has chosen wisely. And you are right," she added, still smiling, "he is quite handsome."

As Anna talked she had finished her kneading and the bread was ready for the oven. Her pride in her indoor oven was justified, and in her bread also, which was considered by all the countryside as the very best. As she finished her task, she looked back at her daughter and saw that once again she was gazing into the courtyard, again lost in thoughts that seemed as far away as the mountains that surrounded the Valley of Jezreel.

The room was quiet except for the sounds made by the clatter of the earthnware as Anna performed her chores.

"Mary, my daughter," the woman's voice interrupted the silence, "I have the table cleared and you may set out the dishes for our supper. First, get the milk from the spring and bring a fresh bucket of water, also."

Mary arose slowly and gracefully to her feet. "Yes, Mother," she answered. "The sun is beginning to disappear, and the wind seems to be stirring in the courtyard. Perhaps, Joseph will come home with Father tonight." She added the last sentence with a hopeful sigh.

And again Anna smiled. "I hope so, child," she said. "I think you are becoming anxious to marry and leave your home."

The girl was immediately alarmed lest she had hurt her mother. "Oh no, Mother. It isn't that at all." Then she saw her mother's smile and smiled herself. "You are teasing me. But, perhaps I am a little overanxious." And she turned and went out into the courtyard where she picked up a bucket made of blackened leather and started for the spring behind the small white limestone house.

The spring, only a few feet from the house, but out of sight of the courtyard, was indeed a luxury and novelty in Nazareth. The common well in the center of the small hamlet was used by all the families for their drinking water and water was not plentiful, but occasionally a small spring from the mountains seemed to bubble up in the valley and it was here that Heli, father of Mary, had built his small house. It was a favorite spot for Mary. Here, as a child, she had played and dreamed alone, or played with her younger sister, Maria. The beautiful old cypress trees kept it always sheltered from the blistering sun in the summer, and although it was only early spring, the sun had been very warm. Mary knelt to secure the milk from its cool hiding place in the water and she let the cool water trickle over her fingers.

Could Joseph have seen Mary at that moment, he would have been even more sure than ever of his love for her. Her dark hair was worn coiled about her head in the usual Jewish fashion, but tiny curls escaped around the nape of her neck. Her black eyes were soft and shining, and her lashes thick and bristly. Her complexion, unlike that of so many of her people, was as white as the marble of the great colonnades that rose in the market places of Jerusalem. Her mouth was sweet and gentle, and her even white teeth sparkled when she smiled. The soft white folds of her gown covered her from her neck to her sandaled feet; not even a toe showed. But the most charming thing about

Mary was that she was never aware of her beauty. She was a simple and forthright as the winds blowing around the Galilean hills. She seemed, as her mother felt, to move always in an inner world more beautiful than the real one in which she lived. There was always just a shadow of reluctance when having to come back to reality.

As she knelt there by the spring, she suddenly saw a reflection of white in the water and was aware that someone was standing just behind her. She was not really afraid, yet she knew no one had immediately followed her, nor had she heard the sound of a footstep. She did not look around for a second, but when she did, she could see the lower part of a man's garment. It was not like any raiment she had ever seen, and her eyes traveled slowly upward to see the rest of him. His eyes were soft, and she felt warm and wonderful as she looked into the face of this stranger. *This is what I have waited for all my life,* she thought.

The man stood very still, and there was about him a sort of light, which did not actually seem to touch his person. When he spoke Mary thought she heard somewhere in the distance a faint sound of thunder. The man's voice was like music and he said, * "Hail, thou art highly favoured; the Lord is with thee: blessed art thou among women."

The man's eyes searched into Mary's, and he saw a troubled look and puzzlement at his words. She was pale and one hand clutched tightly the bucket of milk.

He spoke again, gently, to reassure her, ** "Fear not, Mary, for thou hast found favor with God. And, behold thou shalt conceive in thy womb, and bring forth a son, and thou shalt call his name Jesus. He shall be great, and shall be called the

*Luke 1:26–8
**Luke 1:26–8

4

Son of the Highest, and the Lord God shall give unto him the throne of his father David. And he shall reign over the house of Jacob forever, and of his kingdom there shall be no end."

Mary, knowing that her marriage with Joseph had by no means been settled, and that only the betrothal ceremony had taken place, wondered how this stranger could be so positive and she asked, her voice trembling, * "How shall this be, seeing I know not a man?"

And the man answered, ** "The Holy Ghost shall come upon thee, and the power of the Highest shall overshadow thee; therefore also that which shall be born of thee shall be called the Son of God. And, behold, thy cousin Elizabeth, she hast also conceived a son in her old age; and this is the sixth month with her, who was called barren. For with God nothing shall be impossible."

The full impact of the man's words did not fall on Mary at once, but suddenly she knew that she had been chosen of God for some miraculous reason and she said, "Behold the handmaid of the Lord, be it unto me according to thy word."

She had cast her eyes down as she had spoken, and when she lifted her head, she saw the man had gone. She was not surprised, and somehow she knew he was a messenger from God called Gabriel.

The sun's last glorious rays were making a fiery light behind the hills, and Mary stood very still where she had arisen, her face exalted by her experience with the angel. Time suddenly stood still, the sun, which was sinking rapidly, seemed to wait a moment before leaving the earth in darkness, and suddenly with a little moan, Mary fell to the ground. The trees, in the strange half-light, were like guardians and the gentle

*Luke 1:26–38
**Luke 1:26–38

dusk, a blanket, which covered Mary, and only they were a witness to the miracle of the ages. Only they knew when the Holy Ghost came upon Mary.

Anna, still in the house, felt something stir within her. She felt a rush of wind, and looked up as she thought she heard distant thunder but not a cloud was in the sky, and nothing moved outside. She walked to the door to see the glowing sunset and was about to turn back to her work, but a word of warning tugged at her mind and suddenly she was at the edge of the courtyard, straining her eyes into the glowing sky for the sight of Mary returning from the spring. When she did not see her, Anna called softly, at first, then with a growing sense of fear, loudly. Quickly, she was running in the direction of the spring. She was almost on Mary's still form before she saw her lying on the ground.

"My child, my child," Anna whimpered as she knelt beside her, "what is it? What has happened to you?"

Examining Mary closely Anna found she was still breathing, but her pale face frightened Anna so that she thought surely death was not far away. She gathered the slight girl into her strong arms and made her way back to the house. Through the courtyard and into the warm room where her bread baked in the oven, Anna carried Mary. She paused a moment, looking down into the girl's face, and took her into the room where Mary and her sister slept. She laid her gently down on the couch and immediately began to rub the small, lifeless hands. In a moment or so, Mary stirred and opened her eyes. She was dazed and was not aware her mother was near. Anna spoke softly.

"My child, are you ill?"

"No, Mother," Mary answered, her lips barely moving, and Anna had to lean quite near to hear her answer.

"Did someone frighten you or did you see a serpent or some other animal that frightened you?" Anna's voice showed puzzlement, but relief that Mary could speak.

The girl did not answer at once. When she spoke, however, her voice was more normal, although she still wore the same faraway, dazed look. Her first words were in the form of a question.

"Mother, Mother," she asked earnestly, "do you believe that a Messiah will come to us soon?"

Anna was so startled by the question that she thought surely she must have misunderstood her daughter, but Mary's questioning eyes belied this. Anna was as well-schooled as any Hebrew woman in regard to her promised Messiah, but she seldom gave such things much thought. Her answer to Mary was, therefore, somewhat impatient. "Yes, of course, Mary," she said. "Every Jew knows that God will send a Messiah. And it is hoped that it will be very soon. But why do you ask?"

"I ask, my Mother, because I have been chosen to become the Mother of our Messiah." Mary looked into her mother's eyes and her own were serene and showed no fear, no doubt.

Anna stared into her daughter's face. Her own face showed a mixture of emotions, doubt, fear for her daughter's sanity, sorrow. Yet, something in Mary's eyes stopped her speech. And Anna remembered how strange she had felt but a few moments ago in the kitchen, and then she asked softly, "How do you know this thing, Mary? Why do you think such a thing could happen to you? We are humble, unknown people."

Mary smiled, her eyes luminous with an inner light. "I know not. It seems now almost like a dream." Her mother seemed about to agree, but Mary shook her head.

"No, Mother, it was not a dream. I knelt beside the spring to get the milk, and suddenly a man stood beside me. It was the angel, Gabriel. I do not know his name, for I have never heard it that I remember. But he stood there in shining white raiment."

Then Mary quoted the angel's words about conceiving by the Holy Ghost.

"And then," Mary went on, "the whole world seemed to be listening, the sun to stand still, and I felt that a great wind rushed by me. I remember nothing else until I awoke here with you."

Anna could not breathe. Her heart beat so wildly that she knew it would leap out of her breast. Her hands trembled and she had to clasp them tightly together to hold them steady.

Mary went on, her voice full of emotion. "He said, also, that my cousin, Elizabeth, was in her sixth month."

Anna's startled voice interrupted her daughter. "Elizabeth? But Elizabeth is older than I, my daughter, and has been barren all her life. It has been a great sorrow to her that she could never bear a child. It is impossible that Elizabeth could conceive at her age."

"Gabriel said nothing was impossible with God, Mother," and Mary's statement carried with it such authority that Anna could only nod her head. And she also realized that Mary was no longer a young child but a woman.

Both women sat, lost in their own thoughts, for what seemed a long time. At last Mary spoke again.

"What am I to do, Mother, about Joseph? Will he believe me? Will Father believe me?"

Anna turned pale. She had not thought what Joseph might do. But she spoke soothingly to Mary and said, "I do not know, my child, whether such a thing could be true or not. I love you with all my heart and I find it hard to believe, myself, but this I know. You have been through some wonderful experience and whether you dreamed it or not, I do not know. We will say nothing to Heli tonight. Perhaps in the morning I will have thought of what to say and how to tell him."

"I do not understand it either, Mother. Why I would be chosen for such a miracle is unbelievable, but somehow I know it is true, and that I already carry the Son of God."

9

Anna turned away from Mary quickly so that the tears that had gathered in her eyes could not be seen.

As Anna entered the kitchen, she saw her husband, Heli, and Joseph, Mary's bethrothed, standing in the courtyard talking. Joseph, his carpenter's tools slung over his back, was evidently speaking of something important with Heli before coming into the house. Anna turned to the oven, striving to get herself under control before facing the two men. She was a stocky, comely woman and typically Jewish. Her dark hair was thick and beginning to turn a silvery gray. Her black eyes were clear and set wide apart under the high brow, and usually there was laughter in them, but now a worried look akin to fear had banished that completely.

Joseph spoke to Anna as she turned, with a smile, to greet him. "Anna," he said, "it is good to see you. I trust all has gone well with you since last we met."

"We are well, Joseph." And Anna looked at him with affection. She felt very close to Joseph. Suddenly, she could see him as a little boy again, standing there in the same room so long ago. He had just lost his father, and his mother he had never known. A lost, frightened lad, she remembered, and he had come to her like a baby bird pushed out of his nest too soon, and although he had not made his home with her and Heli, he had spent most of his free time there. And when he was old enough, he had become an apprentice to Heli in the carpenter shop. Anna smiled to herself when she recalled how he had acted when Mary was born. He had become her devoted slave and had announced quite boldly when he was eighteen that he would wait for her to grow up before he married. And, that he had done, but now he was impatient for Heli to set the wedding date.

All these things Anna thought of as she watched him take off the heavy tools from his shoulder, wash his hands in the laver near the door, and seat himself comfortably on the low dais covered with skins.

Joseph was in quite a good humor and asked for Mary when he did not see her about. When told she was not feeling well, he was all concern, as was Heli. However, Anna assured them it was nothing serious and she was asleep, and that it was better not to disturb her. Joseph was disappointed but thought that perhaps Heli would speak about the wedding more readily without Mary present, and became cheered somewhat.

The two men sat down to the fresh bread, honey, and cool milk with relish. There was also cold lamb and several different kinds of fruit. Anna waited on them, as was the custom, and when she saw that their needs were taken care of, and with the evening prayers said, she sat down at a small table nearby to partake of her food.

The two men talked freely of their work, politics, and the activities of the synagogue.

Anna watched them with mixed emotions. *What would they say when she told them of Mary's experience?* she asked herself. "How can I tell them?" she muttered aloud, and blushed when her husband looked across at her from his place at the table with a questioning expression. She shook her head at him and resumed eating.

The men finished their meal and Joseph spoke. "Anna, your bread is fit for Herod's table. If he hears about you, he is likely to make a bargain with Heli for your services in his great kitchens".

"Anna's bread is as good to me, my friend, as it would be to Herod," and Heli smiled affectionally at Anna.

"There is nothing like a good wife," Heli went on, "and nothing like a bad one, either."

Joseph smiled and spoke quietly. "Why don't you set the wedding date for Mary and me, Heli? You know I have waited a long time, and my patience is beginning to run out, I'm afraid."

"I have every intention of speaking, Joseph," and Heli's face became sober and serious. "I am proud and happy to have my Mary marry a man who is like a son to me already, and you may marry Mary anytime you desire. The proper time of the bethrothal has passed. You two have only to state the time."

Joseph rose and reached for Heli's hand. "You make me proud, Heli. I love Mary and I shall cherish her all the days of my life."

Heli turned to Anna with a smile. "Now, if we can give our daughter, Maria, to her Cleophas, my wife, we shall have to look for something to take up all our time."

Anna smiled at her husband, but the smile was forced. Heli knew every expression of his wife's face and he said quickly, "What is it, Anna? Don't you wish Mary and Joseph to marry so soon? I thought it was well with you. They have waited the proper time."

"It is not that, Heli," Anna answered, "I am very proud for Mary to marry Joseph."

Joseph's voice sounded strained as he spoke, still standing, "Is it that Mary does not wish to marry me, Anna? Has she changed her mind?"

"No, Joseph, that is not it. Mary wants to marry you. We were speaking of it only this day." Anna fumbled for words to reassure the men and herself. She had not wished to speak of all this before morning and could find no words. Finally, she mumbled, "It is something personal, Heli, that I must discuss with you. I'm sorry, Joseph, that I could not control myself well enough to keep my husband from seeing my concern until later."

"Anna," Heli's voice commanded her. "Anna, I demand you tell me what this matter is about. If Joseph is to be my son, he should know whatever it is that concerns Mary, if that is what it is. Does it concern my daughter, Mary?"

"Yes, Heli," Anna answered nervously. "Yes, it concerns Mary, Joseph, all of us. But I don't know how to tell you. How to explain it so that you will understand and that Joseph will understand."

Both Joseph and Heli were by now visibly shaken, and Anna's nervousness and reluctance to go on made them very apprehensive.

"What do you know of the coming of the Messiah?" Anna asked, and her voice was low and trembling.

Joseph looked at her, astounded, and sat down slowly on the dais from which he had arisen, and Heli's look plainly showed he thought his wife had gone mad.

"What in heaven's name has the coming of the Messiah got to do with Mary and Joseph?" he thundered.

The overwrought woman jumped at the sound of her husband's voice.

"Everything," she said, tears starting to flow down her face. "Everything. For Mary says she is with child of the Holy Ghost."

Joseph buried his face in his hands, and Heli's ashen face seemed to have turned to stone.

Anna cried silently for a moment. Then she realized that the two men had no understanding of what she had said except that Mary was with child.

She spoke through her tears, but with control. "Heli, you must hear me out."

And Anna told them about Mary's experience with the angel at the spring.

Bewilderment at Anna's words made Heli shake his head. Joseph had pure unbelief on his face.

Anna, looking at Joseph's bowed head, went to him. Putting her arms about his shoulders, she said, gently, "Joseph, you must believe that Mary has never known a man. I promise you that. She may have dreamed all this, but I am sure she is a virgin. She loves you and has waited for you, and you alone, to become her husband."

Anna turned to Heli. "You have never answered me, my husband. Do you know when the expected Messiah of our people is to come and how he is to come?"

Heli answered, slowly. "Only that one has been expected, Anna, for centuries and because of our troubled times, we believe He must have come and save us soon. We have all been taught that He will come from the lineage of David, but I know little else. I do know that it is fantastic that Mary should think she is to bear the Messiah, and I'm surprised that you would listen to such a wild story. She is ill and does not know what she is saying. If she is with child, she must tell us the name of the man at once."

Anna cried out, "No, Heli. She has not known a man. She is with me constantly, and she has never paid the slightest heed to any man save Joseph and you could not, would not, suspect Joseph of such a thing."

Heli turned to Joseph. "I know you are not guilty of such a sin. You do not have to marry Mary, for if she is mad, I would not want marriage for her. If she is not mad, and is with child, you would not want her. I release you from your promises." And he turned away from Joseph and Anna and went to the bedchamber he and Anna shared. They could hear his footsteps as he slowly walked up and down, and Anna thought she detected the faint sound of sobbing, but she could not be sure.

Joseph turned from Anna, picked up his tools, and walked to the door of the courtyard before he spoke.

"I shall return, Anna, to help you in any way I can. I pray to God no harm will come to Mary." And he left, his shoulders sagging under the burden of his tools.

Anna went to Mary's room and saw that she was in a deep

14

sleep. She apparently had heard none of the conversation, and Anna breathed a sigh of relief that Mary had not heard her father's words. She left quickly and tiptoed to her husband's bedside. He did not speak as she sat down beside him. She tried quietly to tell him again about the wonderful look in Mary's eyes, but he would not listen. She told him what Mary had said about Elizabeth, and at that he laughed bitterly.

"Isn't that proof, Anna, that Mary is not herself? She must have made the whole thing up, but why I cannot imagine. And if she is with child, and has fabricated such a story, she will be punished even more severely than if she had told the truth."

"My husband, my husband," Anna childed. "Has all the faith and love you had for your daughter gone to nothing in such a brief moment? Can you have nothing but bitterness and mistrust in your heart for your elder daughter, even is she has gone astray, which I do not believe."

"I do not know, Anna." Heli's voice was softer. "It is just that it seems like a nightmare. For you to announce that Mary was with child was a terrible shock. I am confused. You know I love Mary and will do all I can to protect her. But, Joseph, he is so horribly hurt."

"Yes, I know," Anna answered thoughtfully. "He said he would do all he could, but I do not guess he will marry her now. He did not offer when he left."

"It is getting late, Anna," her husband said, reaching out to touch her face. "You have been through quite a lot yourself, haven't you? But you believe in Mary and perhaps you are right. She has been so good all her life, it is hard to conceive of her doing wrong. We shall not worry tonight, and maybe with the day, it will straighten itself out. Perhaps if it has been a dream, or an illness, it will have passed away. She may have forgotten it by morning. Come to bed." And Heli turned his face to look out the window at the beauty of the night. A moon had risen,

15

and the whole earth looked like a great lake of light. The white, chalklike hills were dazzling.

Anna, getting ready for bed quietly in the darkened room, wondered many things about her husband.

Could she convince him that Mary was to bear the Messiah, if such a miracle could have happened? Would he allow Mary to stay in their home, unmarried, while she carried the child? And suddenly cold fear clutched her heart. She suddenly remembered the terrible punishment accorded a woman bearing a child out of wedlock. Mary would be stoned to death under the law. Anna's hands shook and as she lay down beside Heli, she felt that sleep would be a long way off, but she was exhausted with the day's labors and the emotional experience she had been through, and sleep came quickly.

The same moonlight that flooded the room where Anna and Heli slept surrounded Joseph like the pale satin of a robe. The beauty of the night seemed to mock him. His dreams of the lovely Mary had shattered into a million pieces, and each piece seemed to gleam through the trees. Eveywhere he looked he could see her soft, sweet smile, and pain tore at his heart until he felt it would burst.

"How could she do such a thing?" he said aloud. "She knows I love her, and I was so sure she loved me. I have seen her answering look many times when my eyes questioned her." And Joseph almost sobbed aloud.

As he neared the house where he lived with an old uncle, a brother of Joseph's father, he could see the man sitting out under a tree in the small courtyard. Joseph did not want to talk with anyone and so he stood in the shadow of the white wall for a long time, lost in thought, waiting for the man to retire. Doubts and fears darted in and out of his mind. He tried hard not to believe that Mary's child, if there was one, was not that of another man. But his practical mind would not accept the story that the child was the Son of God.

"Maybe," he whispered to himself, "maybe she dreamed it all and she isn't going to have a child after all."

Weariness overcame him and he realized that he had been standing under the tree for a long time and that the old man had gone into the house. He walked slowly to his bedchamber. As Joseph lay down on his bed, fully clothed, too weary to remove even his outer garment, he closed his eyes but not in sleep. How long he lay there he did not know, but suddenly the room seemed filled with a peculiar light and he opened his eyes. He seemed to hear the sound of distant thunder, and then he felt the presence of someone in the room. His eyes beame accustomed to the brilliant light, and he saw, standing at the side of his bed, a man in shining white raiment.

Joseph was terrified, yet fascinated by the man's presence, and when the visitor spoke, Jospeh let out a deep sigh and realized he had been holding his breath.

The man said, * "Joseph, fear not to take Mary as your wife. That which she is to bear is of the Holy Ghost. Protect and cherish her, for she is most honored of women."

Before Joseph could speak, the man seemed to fade away rather than just vanish, and the light in the room dimmed until the glow of the moon was all that was left. He lay still for a long time. He did not know whether he had dreamed or whether he had seen a vision, but he knew that whichever it was, it had been a message from God. He, like Mary, knew the messenger had been Gabriel. He was stirred as never before. A peace overcame him, and he knew his whole life had changed in those few minutes. He, Joseph, was to guard the Mother of the Saviour of his people. He longed for morning so he could go to her and tell her all was well. Sleep finally came, however, and the sun was high when he awoke.

*Matthew 1:20

Leaping from bed he changed his clothes quickly. The dream or vision he had had was still as fresh as the morning, and he could remember every detail. As he left his room, his uncle stopped him to tell him the morning meal was about ready, but Joseph impatiently told him he could not eat as he had an important errand to perform. He left his uncle abruptly and without further explanation. He almost ran down the road leading to Heli's home, dazzling in the early morning sunshine, and thought he could see movement in the courtyard.

As he came to the entrance, he saw Mary sitting on a small stone bench by the door. Her face was sweet, yet sad, and she was lost in thought. He was almost upon her when she heard his footsteps and turned to look up into his face. It was evident she had heard of last night's conversation between Joseph and her father, and her face was one of bewilderment and sadness as she looked into Joseph's eyes. It turned from bewilderment, however, to joy at what she saw there, and a smile flooded her face when she saw he was smiling temderly at her.

"Mary," he said gently. "Mary, my little brave woman. I am most proud and humble in your sight. I do not pretend to understand all of this, but I am most happy that I am to have some part in so great a miracle."

"Oh, Joseph," Mary's voice shook with emotion, and tears of gladness ran down her cheeks. "You do understand then. You will have faith in me."

"Yes, Mary," Joseph answered. "Last night I had a vision also, and I am very ashamed that I ever doubted you for a moment. I shall try to make up for any doubts or fears I may have had, and I hope to make you very happy. Please marry me at once, today if you will."

Joseph reached out, took Mary's hand in his, and pulled her gently into his arms and held her. He kissed the top of her head and her forehead tenderly while she cried quietly in his arms.

Heli and Anna, hearing voices in the courtyard, came to the door just in time to see Joseph take Mary into his arms. They were stunned at the expression on Joseph's face, for there was no doubting the love and devotion, faith and happiness written there.

Heli spoke first. "Joseph, my son. You make us very happy. You are indeed a fine man to overlook this thing that has happened to Mary and are willing to forgive her."

Joseph turned angry eyes to Heli and spoke with such vehemence that Heli recoiled from him. "Heli, you must believe in Mary. I am making no sacrifice to want her as my wife. Last night a messenger of God came to me in a dream and rebuked me for my lack of faith in this most honored woman. Mary is to bear the Messiah for our people, and we must believe and protect her."

Mary spoke quickly. "Did Gabriel come to you also, Joseph? Did he really? Please tell me I am not mistaken, and that I did really talk with him and am to bear the Son of God."

"He did come to me, in shining white raiment, just as he came to you," Joseph answered, "and you need have no doubts, no fear that you are mistaken. He told me to take you as my wife and protect you until your son is born. I shall do so without further delay, if you and your father are willing."

"Joseph," Heli said, "I am most ashamed. Forgive me, Mary, my daughter. Your mother and I are just simple people and all this is more than we can understand, but we will try. You both have our blessing, and you have our permission to marry at once."

There were tears of joy and relief in Anna's eyes, and the others stood and looked at Mary as she turned her sweet smile on them.

"I would like to marry Joseph as soon as my sister, Maria, has returned from her visit to my cousin Elizabeth."

Each of the trio nodded in agreement, and Anna turned

back into the kitchen, saying, "Come, we shall have food and discuss plans for the wedding."

Heli, following Anna, spoke in a low voice to her. "I am most relieved, Anna, and I think that now no one will know about Mary's strange experience. Joseph will protect her, and people will think the child is his son.

Anna looked at him for a moment and started to speak. Then she realized that argument was useless. Perhaps he was right and perhaps it would be better for Mary that people think the child was Joseph's. She did not know what Mary would say to others about this thing. How she wished Mary could go away for a little while after she married Joseph. She would have a talk with both of them after their meal. Right now she must think of getting the food prepared, and she busied herself with the task.

Mary went about getting the dishes on the table for the men, and room was quiet except for the low voices of Heli and Joseph as they talked at the other side of the room. They were talking, no doubt about Mary, but she seemed oblivious of it and went about setting the table mechanically, her thoughts many miles away.

After the men had eaten heartily, Mary and Anna joined them and Heli spoke.

"Maria should arrive today. Two of Cleophas's men rode ahead of the caravan and arrived yesterday. We are safe, I'm sure, to set the wedding for the day after tomorrow. Even if the caravan is delayed, it will not be more than a day or so. They should certainly be here by that time."

When he finished speaking, Heli looked at Mary for confirmation. She nodded her head in agreement. "Yes, I am sure she will be here by that time. If Joseph is agreeable to those plans, I am pleased."

Joseph smiled at Mary and said, "I have waited all my life

21

for you, my dear, so the day after tomorrow couldn't be too soon."

Then Anna spoke. "We must settle something else, also, my children. The child Mary carries is not Joseph's. The neighbors and relatives will naturally think it is. This is a most delicate matter, and we have to decide whether or not we are to let them think this or tell them about Mary's experience and that she will bear the Messiah."

Heli spoke quickly before Mary could speak. "They must not to be told about it. They will not believe it but think that Joseph had Mary before marriage or that the child is someone else's. This way they will never know but that the child was conceived after their marriage. There will be no scandal, and I believe God wanted to have it that way or he would not have come to Joseph in a dream as he did."

Mary was pale. "But the child is not Joseph's, Father, and it will be deceiving the people to allow them to think so. How will they know the Messiah has come if they think the child is just another child?"

Anna spoke quietly to Mary. "God will find a way, Mary. You must not concern yourself. I have been thinking that perhaps you and Joseph should go away for a little while after your wedding. If Joseph had his own home to take you to, it would not be necessary, but living with Elias and Rebecca will not be easy for you. If you could visit with some relative, perhaps when you returned, Heli and I will have some plan for your living quarters. Perhaps you could live here with us."

Anna's conversation was interrupted by a commotion in the courtyard. The sound of laughter and voices floated through the kitchen door, and as the four people sitting around the table arose to greet the guests, Maria appeared in the doorway.

Maria was taller than Mary and was the exact opposite in that she seemed to ooze vitality. She was vivacious, and laughter

23

seemed always trembling on her lips and in her eyes even when she tried to be sober and serious. People smiled when she passed by, and she was in a constant good humor. She loved to be moving around, and visiting friends and relatives was her greatest joy. She loved her family, however, and was always glad to get back in the family circle. In a moment she had embraced her mother, father, and Mary and had spoken gaily to Joseph.

Cleophas, to whom Maria was bethrothed, stood in the doorway, awaiting his turn to greet her family. He was a trader of goods, and his caravans were well known in Galilee.

Cleophas brought the necessities as well as luxuries to the people of Nazareth and, though young, had been very success-ful in his business. He was tall and slender and someday when he matured he would be a very large man. He was only part Jew, his mother having been a Greek, and he had inherited her coloring instead of his father's. His blond curly hair always attracted attention among so many dark people. He was quiet and watched Maria in her exuberance with a tolerant smile. It was said that Cleophas was the only person alive who had a restraining effect on Maria.

Two men of the caravan interrupted the family's conver-sation by bringing in Maria's bags and various parcels. She showed them the way to hers and Mary's bedchamber, and Cleophas had a chance to speak to Heli and Joseph about the journey from Elizabeth's. They had encountered no difficulties and had made extremely good time.

After the men of the caravan had taken their leave and Maria had returned, the family and their guests settled down to talk for a few minutes before Joseph and Heli set off to work.

Heli spoke, asking Maria, "How did you leave your cousin Elizabeth and Zachariah? Are they well and does all go well in the Temple?"

Maria glanced at Cleophas before she spoke, as though she asked permission to answer her father. He nodded at her and she said, "They are well, Father, except that a most amazing thing has happened. Elizabeth is with child."

The silence of the room became so noticeable that finally Maria said, "I know it is almost unbelieveable at Elizabeth's age, but she was three months with child when I arrived. Zachariah, it seems, saw a vision and an angel."

She was interrupted by Mary's voice, low and trembling with emotion. "The angel Gabriel, Maria."

Maria's eyes were very large as they looked at Mary. "Yes, Mary, the angel, Gabriel. But how did you know? He told Zachariah that he was to have a son by Elizabeth, but Zachariah doubted the angel, and Gabriel told him he would be unable to speak until the birth of the child. He has to write down everything he wants known. He stays in the Temple, praying, almost constantly. The child, the angel said, would be great in the sight of the Lord and would be filled with the Holy Ghost. They are greatly excited about the child. Elizabeth is so happy that she does not even complain about the illness she has been through. She is confident that the child will be born healthy and that she nor the child will suffer any ill effects. I hated to leave her, but I had promised to come home at the end of three months and she made me keep that promise."

Both Heli and Anna were strangely silent. Heli's face was a study—even Joseph's expression was that of bewilderment. Heli was the first to break the silence.

"The Lord doth work in strange ways, my children. Your sister Mary has also been visited by the angel Gabriel, Maria. She is to bear the Messiah the world waits for. He told her that Elizabeth was with child, but we could not believe it. We doubted, in fact, your sister's story, and I am ashamed to say, we thought she had sinned. Joseph, however, was visited by the angel last night, and came this morning to ask that he might marry Mary at once. He has been told to protect her, and they are getting married the day after tomorrow. Now you come with this astounding news of Elizabeth and Zachariah. I am convinced completely—no doubts—no fears."

Maria said quietly, "I would never have doubted her."

Mary smiled lovingly at Maria, then said, "I must go to Elizabeth at once, my father. We have much to say to one another. Mother's suggestion that we go somewhere is taken care of, if Joseph will consent to go."

"I am quite willing, Mary, to go with you to Elizabeth's," Joseph said. "However, you must remember that now we shall be married, and I have to take care of you in more ways than one. My work with your father cannot be left for long."

"Do not fret yourself about the work, Joseph," Heli stated firmly. "I will take care of the carpentry shop until you return. That settles it as far as I'm concerned. You and Mary will leave immediately following the wedding for Judea."

Heli was interrupted by Maria's voice. She had been whispering to Cleophas, and now, looking excitedly at her mother and father, she asked, "Father, please, may Cleophas and I get married at the same time Mary and Joseph do, please?"

Anna had to laugh at the pleading tone of Maria's voice and even Heli was smiling. "Now, now," he said, "two daughters at the time getting married. That's too much to ask of any man."

Cleophas spoke, quietly. "Sir, I would like to add my pleas. Maria and I have waited for Mary to marry first before we asked your permission to have our wedding. It would be most unusual for sisters to marry at the same time."

Heli looked at Anna. Their eyes met and their thoughts seemed to fuse. Heli turned back to the expectant face of Maria.

"All right, Maria, you and Cleophas may have your wedding. Maybe, Maria, you won't be running around the country quite so much now. I think perhaps it is time for you to settle down."

Maria impulsively flung her arms around her father, then

26

her mother. Pulling Mary up out of her place near Joseph, she said, "Come, Mary, let us get ready for our wedding. Our robes must be made ready and guests invited. We must gather flowers. Oh, there are dozens of things to be done and only a few hours to do them in. Come, Mary, come."

Both girls left the room with arms entwined, and the men's eyes followed them with fondness. Anna's eyes were full of sadness as she saw her daughters leave the room. She felt they were, at that moment, leaving her forever. She rose with a sigh and followed them.

Joseph and Heli gathered up Heli's tools. Joseph had forgotten his in his rush to get to Mary earlier that morning. Cleophas left with them to take his caravan into town where he would barter his goods. They could hear the sound of the chattering girls and the subdued tones of their mother's voice as they left, and each smiled at the other.

II

The day of the wedding dawned early, and the sun bathed the land of Galilee in streaks of color. The limestone hills were softened in the beauty of the morning light, and both girls woke very early. Mary, lying still and watching the sun come up through the window, was thinking how many times she had been awakened by the sound of the birds, her mother bustling around in the kitchen or by Maria's laughter. She would miss the quiet happiness of this home where she was born, her parents, who had always been so wonderfully kind and helpful to her, and the gay sister she loved so much. She hoped that perhaps she and Joseph could return and live with her Heli and Anna. There wouldn't be the problem of room now that Maria was leaving to live in Cleophas's home and she was certain her mother wanted her back here. Her thoughts were interrupted by Maria's voice.

"Mary," said Maria, "we must get up and sew the institas on all our robes. You will have no other time, as you are leaving today for Elizabeth's."

The instita, a band worn around the bottom of the robe of a married woman, was most important to Maria. She wished all the world to know she had married Cleophas, and she could hardly wait to don a robe with the instita.

Mary turned over and smiled at Maria. "All right, Maria. We will get them done early because the wedding ceremony is not long in coming."

The girls arose and, filling the laver with water from a pitcher, they washed their faces and put on a long robe over their sleeping garments. Each tied her hair back with a ribbon

and when they appeared in the kitchen, Anna, taking her baking out of the oven, looked up at them and smiled.

"You look more like two little girls dressed up in their mother's clothes than women about to become married today," she said. "You are up early, and Mary, do you feel well, my daughter? You look pale. Perhaps you should have stayed in bed a little longer."

"I am all right, Mother," Mary answered. "I feel quite well. Maria and I are up to sew the institas on our robes, and I must get my clothes ready for travel."

After their meal the girls helped clear up the dishes and straighten the room. The food preparations for the wedding had been done the day before and neighbors and relatives were contributing to this feast and would deliver their shares a little later on in the morning.

The girls returned to their room with their mother, and laid on their beds all their outer garments that would have the instita sewn on them. All three sewed quickly, and there was much chatter about the simple marriage ceremony that would be performed. Maria was much excited about going to live in the house of Cleophas. His parents were not wealthy people, but they had done rather well as trade merchants, and their home was much above the average one in Nazareth. Cleophas and Maria were to have an apartment all to themselves and a servant of their own. They would eat with the family, and Maria was looking forward to living a life of ease, as she called it.

Both Mary and her mother smiled at her, and their laughter from time to time could be heard by passersby, who knowing what they were probably doing, smiled in understanding.

It was not long before neighbors and relatives began coming to bring food and wine for the wedding feast, and Anna left the girls to complete their tasks, to greet and help these kind friends and kin. Great trays of fruit, nuts, and sweets were arranged in beautiful arrays on the tables. Every woman had brought her finest cups and goblets, and indeed the feast would be a sumptuous one. The wedding was to take place just before noon, and a canopy of white had been arranged in the courtyard for the brides and grooms to stand beneath. The ceremony would not be lengthy and then the guests would enter the house and partake of the food.

The morning passed quickly, and almost before Mary and Maria realized it, they were dressed in their robes and veils awaiting Joseph and Cleophas. The Jewish ceremony was carried out to the letter, and Mary and Maria were sober and serious as they listened to the words that bound them to their husbands.

At the end of the ceremony, Mary unfastened Maria's veil and Maria unfastened Mary's, and their husbands were able to see their radiant smiles.

There was much laughter and gaiety during the feast that followed. People stood in small groups, talking with one another and calling greetings to other groups and to the brides and grooms.

Joseph and Mary had not told their plans to anyone except Maria and Cleophas and Mary's parents, and when, later in the afternoon, Mary appeared in the courtyard ready for travel, everyone was aghast. There was much chatter with many questions, and when they learned that Elizabeth was to bear a child and that Mary and Joseph were going to her and stay through her confinement, they were even more surprised.

After Mary and Joseph had taken leave of Heli and Anna, Maria and Cleophas, and their guests, they walked to Joseph's home where they would pick up Joseph's clothes, gather the donkey on which the baggage had been strapped and the donkey on which Mary would ride. Joseph picked up Mary's two small bags to be added to his, and they waved toward the house until they were out of the sight.

"Are you all right, Mary?" Joseph asked tenderly after they had walked the short distance to Joseph's home.

"Oh, yes, Joseph. Do not concern yourself with my feelings. I feel quite well and happy."

He smiled down at her and thought how very delicate and frail she looked in her white robe with the veil thrown back.

"We will not travel long today," Joseph went on. "We'll stop at the inn at Nein, then get a fresh start in the morning before the sun gets hot."

Joseph had only to lead the donkeys out of the stable. The old man and woman with whom he lived were at the wedding feast, and Mary waited for him in the courtyard. She stood, thinking how really changed her life was, and yet she did not feel any different. Here she was married and bearing a child not her husband's, and yet the world went on about her as usual. Suddenly she had an impulse to run and hide from everyone or to sob uncontrollably.

She did neither as she saw Joseph coming from the stable. He waved to her, and she felt his strength and calm manner stealing over her even at that distance. He was by her side in a moment with the two gray donkeys, all ready for the journey. And Mary laughed aloud at the sight of the sturdy little animals looking so serious, for Joseph had tied ribbon bows all over the harness of one of them and on his tail. Little bells tucked into the bows tinkled every time he stepped, and Mary was so delighted that all sadness and fear left her.

Joseph lifted her onto the donkey's back, and she could not speak for laughing at the bows and bells.

"Who did it, Joseph?" she asked when she finally stopped laughing. She was stunned when he answered.

"I did, Mary. I thought perhaps it would amuse you on the long journey."

"It was a wonderful idea, Joseph. And thank you for thinking of it. I'll never forget your doing it for me."

Joseph blushed but looked extremely pleased and stored away in his mind the incident so that he could repeat something similar for her pleasure in the future.

They went along the road for some time in silence except for the tiny little bells tinkling, Joseph leading the donkeys, and Mary sitting looking at the sky.

"When you are tired, Mary," Joseph said, breaking the silence, "be sure you tell me and we'll stop and rest. I am used to much exercise, but you are not."

"I am enjoying the scenery, Joseph. You know I am not like Maria and have never done much traveling. I have not visited Elizabeth since early childhood."

Mary was quiet again for quite a long time, then said, "Joseph, I have had very little time to talk with you since the visit of the angel Gabriel. It seems like months instead of only a few days ago. I am very curious about the child I am to bear and what kind of child it will be. I had always thought of the Messiah coming as a King, not a child. There are so many things I should know. I am not well educated enough to rear a child who will rule the entire universe. My people and yours are simple people, good, but not brilliant, nor wise about the world affairs, and I should think that the child should have to know everything."

She paused and Joseph said, "I think, Mary, that all that will be shown to us. I have thought much about this strange thing, also, and my part in it. Have thought of nothing else. There is something I think I should tell you also to put your mind at rest. I would like you to know how I feel about you, now."

Mary looked up at Joseph as he spoke and thought how kind his face looked. She didn't believe Joseph had ever had an evil thought, and she was glad that he would be near to help her with the child, Jesus. "Please go on, Joseph," she said.

"I have loved you since you were a little girl," he started

33

simply. "When you were a very small child, I thought of you, naturally, as a very dear little girl who was the daughter of the man to whom I owe a great deal. I felt like a brother to you for a good many years. Then one day I realized that you were growing into a very lovely woman, and that my feelings were changing. I was in love with you by the time you had reached your girlhood and have wanted nothing more than for you to grow up so I could ask you to become my wife."

Tears stood in Mary's eyes, for she knew Joseph was a very reticent man and that this speech he was making was taking a great deal of courage on his part. He was not used to revealing his deep emotions in this manner.

His voice dropped into almost a whisper, and she had to lean very close to his shoulder to hear the rest of what he was saying. He looked straight ahead so she could not see his eyes, but she knew how they looked and she placed her hand gently on his shoulder.

Joseph continued, "Although our marriage ceremony was performed this morning, Mary, I shall ask nothing of you until after your son is born. You shall live in peace until that time. In addition to the love I have for you as a man, I am awed by something in your face that is far beyond me. I know I have no part of you as a woman for the time being. I am not unhappy about it, and I want you to know I feel both humble and honored to be your husband. If, for the sake of our reputations, you think it best we share the same bedchamber, we shall do so. That will be up to you. You may wish to be alone, and it will be all right with me if you desire it."

"Oh, Joseph, you are so kind and thoughtful." Mary's voice broke tearfully.

Joseph stopped the donkeys and Mary laid her head against Joseph's chest. He had one arm about her and held her close to him.

"There, little Mary," he said. "Do not concern yourself. I

would not be much of a man if I did not feel this way. I'm making no great sacrifice for you—it is the other way around."

Mary looked up into his face and smiled. "You are the kindest man in the world, Joseph. I love you very dearly. We shall, not for appearance's sake, but because I want very much to share the same bedchamber with you, and we shall be happy. Someday I shall give you sons, and daughters, also. I have been chosen for this wonderful thing by God, but I am, after all, only a woman."

They smiled at one another like any newly married couple, and he leaned and kissed her softly on the lips before he started the little donkeys on their journey.

They reached Nein long before sundown and were settled in the small inn before time for the evening meal. Mary was a little tired, and Joseph made her lie down while he went in search of the innkeeper to arrange for their supper.

The innkeeper, upon learning that Joseph and Mary had married only that day, was very pleased to arrange a small room for their privacy at supper. He would, he said, take care of everything. Their supper would be quite special, and Joseph left it in his hands. He wandered about the streets for a while, looking in the two or three small shops and found in one of them a very slender gold chain with a tiny flower made of a blue stone. It was very dainty and delicately made and it was, he thought, just the thing for Mary. After his purchase he found he wanted to hurry back to the inn to give it to her. He felt a surge of pride and delight in taking a gift to his wife. If he had not felt it would be undignified, he would have run every step of the way. Even now people turned to look at him as he walked quickly along the street. He did not know that his face revealed his feelings and that there was a smile on his lips.

He knocked lightly on the door, and Mary answered him at once. She was not asleep but was still lying down as he opened the door.

"Joseph," she said, as he entered, "you look so pleased about something. What have you been doing?"

Joseph sat down beside her on the couch and handed her the little chain, which he had in his closed hand. The little blue flower gleamed up at her.

"Oh," she cried in delight. "Oh, Joseph, it is beautiful. I am so pleased." She reached up and put her hand on his face. "You are indeed a most wonderful husband."

Joseph blushed with pleasure at her words, and then he told her about the little supper.

"I must," she said "put on another robe. One with an insita on it so that all the inn will know we are married."

Again Joseph flushed with pleasure at her simple delight in being his wife, and he helped her to rise from the bed. As she took her robe from the small bag he had brought up for her, he went to the window and looked out. She changed quickly and when she had finished, she walked up behind him. She handed him the chain and asked, "Will you fasten it for me?"

Joseph put the chain around her neck and raised up the dark curls to fasten it. She waited patiently while his large fingers fumbled with the catch and finally had it fastened. She turned to show him the necklace, and he stood and looked at her. She made a lovely picture in the beautiful robe with the wide blue band around the bottom and the tiny blue flower gleaming on the snow-white robe covering her lovely bosom. Her eyes were shining with excitement and pleasure, and yet there was a detached, ethereal look about her at the same time. Joseph felt a lump rise in his throat and said, with deep emotion. "Mary, my wife."

And she answered with the same emotion showing her her voice. "Joseph, my husband."

"What a wonderful choice you are to bear the Messiah, Mary. At this moment I believe you are the most beautiful person I have ever beheld. I feel that I am in the very presence of God as I think what it is you are to be."

Mary bowed her head, as though in silent prayer for a moment. Then she looked up at him and said, "Thank you for the faith you have in me. I shall need it. I feel, more than you know."

Together they walked across the room, and Joseph opened the door for her to go ahead of him. At the top of the stairs, a lantern had been lit and in the glow of the light, Mary stood for a moment, waiting for Joseph to close the door of their room. Several men below looked up to see her standing there in the light and there was, for a moment, a peculiar silence over the room where there had been raucous laughter a moment before. As she decended the steps with Joseph, their eyes followed her down. The innkeeper, noting the silence, looked up and went to them as they came into the large public room. He showed them to a small private dining room and closed the door. As he went back into the public room, a young soldier ventured to ask, "Who was that, innkeeper?"

"Newly married pair," the innkeeper said wisely, with a big wink. "Why?"

The man breathed easier, it seemed. "Nothing," he said. "For a moment she startled me. There was something about her—well, I can't explain it, something eerie, as though she wasn't one of this world."

"You've had one too many, friend," the innkeeper said laughingly. "They were married in Nazareth today. His name is Joseph and she is Mary, the daughter of Heli the carpenter. Just plain folks. Nothing remarkable about her except she is a pretty wench."

The man who had spoken looked thoughtful for a moment, then turned back to his fellow guests and they began their conversation where they had left off. They were soon laughing and joking again and forgot Mary and Joseph.

The innkeeper had done very well with the supper he had prepared for Mary and Joseph. They were both hungry after the journey, and they had eaten very little of the wedding feast. Joseph watched with pleasure as Mary ate, and he was glad to see that she had suffered no illness as yet from her pregnancy. He had always been aware of her excellent health despite her fragile appearance.

Joseph ate heartily also, and when they had finished, they walked in the garden back of the little inn. A beautiful moon could be seen nestling in the clouds, but it would be hours before it would be up. Joseph knew they had a long journey, ahead and before long, he suggested they go up to their bedchamber. Mary agreed and they walked slowly back to the inn and through the public room.

Joseph put his arm protectively around Mary as they started to the stairs. He knew the men there had been drinking heavily and that they might make remarks about Mary, knowing she was a new bride. He was surprised that complete silence greeted their entrance and not even a laugh sounded in the room as they ascended the stairs. He realized suddenly there was something about Mary's appearance that made them hold their laughter and conversation and that they had done so when she descended the stairs. He looked at her reverently as she walked quietly by his side to the door of their room. He opened it and she passed inside without a glance at the room below. He closed the door quickly, relieved that she had not had to endure any rough conversation and that she was unaware that such a danger had existed.

"Her innocence," he said to himself, "is protection in itself."

A small silken screen stood in one corner of the room, and Joseph pulled it over the floor so that a small corner was shut off from the rest of the room. He moved Mary's small trunk behind this, filled her laver with water, and put it on a small

table by the side of the trunk. She watched him as he moved about the room arranging things for her privacy, and he caught her smiling at him when he had finished.

"You are being so thoughtful and taking such care of me, Joseph, that I am beginning to feel spoiled."

He laughed with pleasure but said nothing, and she walked behind the screen to prepare for bed.

When she walked out, attired in her wedding night dress, with her beautiful dark hair hanging around her shoulders, she looked very young and lovely. Her heart, she knew, was beating very fast and instead of its usual pallor, her face was pink.

As she stepped from behind the screen, Joseph noticed her tiny bare feet. He suddenly went to her, picked her up in his strong arms, and carried her to the bed. He put her down tenderly and pulled the light coverlet over her, then went behind the screen to undress and prepare for bed himself.

Mary's heart still beat like a small hammer, and she felt sure Joseph could hear it behind the screen. Suddenly the room was thrown into darkness, and she realized Joseph had blown out the candle. Through the open window, she could see the tip of the moon over a fluffy cloud. She heard Joseph's tread across the room, and he silently got into the bed next to her.

She felt as though she could not breathe and realized she was holding her breath. He lay quietly beside her for some time, and she began to breathe more normally and relax the tense muscles of her arms and shoulders. Her mind began to function again, and suddenly she knew what an effort Joseph was making for her sake. Here was a man who loved her as any man loved a bride but was unable to make any overtures of love. She timidly sought his hand, and when she found it, he took her small hand in his. He turned over and touched her face gently, and in a moment, she was in his arms and he was holding her close, tenderly and protectively. She went to sleep there in his arms and it was not long before Joseph, too, was asleep. And so it was that Joseph took unto him, Mary, his wife, and knew her not until Jesus was born.

III

The stars were still shining brightly when Joseph awoke. The air was cool, and through the window, he could see the blue-black sky, and the tops of the trees moving made a low singing sound. He lay very still, so as not to disturb Mary, until the sky began to brighten a little. Then he cautiously got out of bed and, without putting on his shoes, dressed himself and after placing his night clothes in his bag, he quietly let himself out the door. The inn was still, except for the snores of some of the fellow travelers, and he did not expect to see the landlord up and about as he descended the stairs.

"Well, sir," the landlord said, looking up at him coming down the stairs, "you are indeed an early riser."

"Yes," Joseph answered. "My wife and I have to travel while it is cool, and we have a long way to go yet. I wonder if I could get some milk and cheese for our breakfast. I would like to eat mine here, then take my wife's to her."

The landlord looked at Joseph in unbelief. "You want to take your wife's breakfast to her?" he asked. "Is she ill?"

"Of course not," Joseph answered somewhat sternly. "It is very early, and my wife will be very tired before the day is over. I am letting her rest as long as possible."

"The practice is not done here, sir," the landlord answered. "But you are welcome to do whatever you please. I'll get your milk and cheese and serve you here. Would you like some hot bread just from the oven?"

"I would, indeed, and honey if you have some," Joseph replied. "While you set it here, I'll see to my donkeys." And he walked out with his bag into the yard.

The landlord watched him go with a shake of his head.

"Odd man, that one. Doesn't look like a man who would serve his wife's breakfast to her." Then he laughed loudly. "Why, bless me, of course, he is a bridegroom and probably wants an excuse to keep her in bed as long as possible."

The crude fellow went to fetch the food, and when Joseph came back, his breakfast was waiting. Also, a tray for Mary was on the table, covered with a cloth. Joseph had in his hand a small flower he had picked by the side of the doorway, and he lifted the cover on the tray and laid it on the plate by the hot bread. He then picked up the tray and went quietly up the steps. The landlord had been watching with interest the placing of the flower on the plate, and when Joseph picked up the tray and left with it before touching his own breakfast, the landlord was amazed. He watched further as Joseph quietly opened the door of their room at the top of the stairs. In less than two minutes, he was further amazed to see Joseph descending the stairs and sitting down to eat his breakfast.

Mary had heard Joseph opening the door to bring in her tray, and in the half-light of the room, she saw he was dressed. When he approached the bed, she spoke to him.

"Good morning, Joseph." She saw him smile.

"Good morning, Mary," he said gently. "I've brought your breakfast. I thought perhaps it would be better than to have to eat in the public room below. The landlord is a crude fellow, and besides that, you have a long journey ahead of you."

Mary sat up and looked up into his face with eyes full of tears. She smiled sweetly, too full of emotion to answer.

Joseph uncovered the tray and set it on the bed, propping her pillow behind her back. When he had finished, he looked back into her face and saw her tender smile as she picked up the rose and held it to her lips in a soft kiss.

"Thank you, my husband," was all she said.

"When you have done with your food and have dressed," Joseph said, "call me and I will come up for you. I'll be down

44

in the public room having my food. The donkeys are ready, and we must leave so as to be able to travel before the sun gets too hot. I will ask the landlord for our midday meal, for we may be a long way from an eating place." And he kissed her gently on the forehead and left.

Mary found she was hungry. She ate all the bread and cheese and drank the fresh milk with relish. She was dressed soon after, with her rose tucked in her dark hair. She put on a dark cloak, as it was still quite cool outside, and opened the door to call Joseph. As she stepped out into the hall, the young soldier who had noticed her the night before came out of a room that housed about ten men. He was rather disheveled looking, and upon seeing Mary, he stopped suddenly and stared at her. Her beautiful, serene eyes caught his and for a moment held him in her glance. Then she dropped her eyes and walked to the top of the stairs where she could see Joseph paying the landlord and receiving their prepared food. She called down to him softly, and he looked up to see the young soldier descending the stairs. The soldier kept looking back at Mary with such a puzzled expression on his face that for a moment Joseph was about to ask if something was wrong. But, apparently nothing was, from Mary's expression, and she had eyes only for Joseph.

Joseph bounded up the steps, got the rest of their belongings from their room, and they both went down together and out the door into the yard without further comment.

The landlord and soldier stood watching them for several moments. Even after they had gone from view, the two men stood, each lost in thought.

The landlord finally spoke. "Most unusual pair, those two. He took her morning food up to her and came down and had his own. And they just married yesterday."

The soldier, still staring into the yard, said, "She looks so unreal, like something might have happened to her that never has happened before."

The landlord laughed crudely. "Nothing happened to her that hasn't happened to every bride, my boy," and he was stunned when the young man turned on him in anger.

"Shut up, you boor. Is nothing sacred to you?"

"Well," the landlord said, in a huff, "you've been staying here for a long time and that's the first time I've ever heard you say anything about a girl being 'sacred,' and he stormed out of the room.

The soldier sat down at the table and stared into space until the servant appeared with his meal. In his mind the young man could see Mary sitting on the donkey, her beautiful calm face looking toward the sky or smiling gently at Joseph. "I'll never forget that face," he said to himself silently, "and I hope to see her again sometime."

The soldier had no idea that he would see her again at the foot of a cross—her beautiful calm face looking up at her son—and he had never forgotten her face.

Mary and Joseph were silent for a long time, Joseph leading the two donkeys and Mary sitting on one listening to the tiny tinkling bells. It was a happy silence, and each was content to be with the other. Each was thinking how wonderful the other was, and Joseph was very much aware of his deep responsibility for Mary and this child she was bearing. He knew that Mary was going to worry very much when the child came because people would think her son was his, Joseph's. And yet, to protect her and the child, they had to think it, for they would not believe it was the Son of God. They would laugh at her, mock and ridicule her and him. They would call him a fool if he denied he was the father of this child, and most of all, they would make the child's life miserable. He sighed, deeply, and Mary heard him.

"What is it, Joseph?" she asked. "Are you tired? If so, please let us rest."

"No, Mary," he answered. "I'm not tired. I was just

thinking about our problems with this child. You and I know that it is God's Son. Your mother and father believe it, and Maria and Cleophas believe it, because your mother and father believe it."

Mary interrupted him, gently, "Joseph, you must not concern yourself. Since I have been selected to bear the child, I know that God will find a way to protect us all. It is too wonderful and great a thing for me to doubt that the plan has been made and will be completed by God."

She smiled into his face and he was reassured. "You are right, of course. I have no right to question so great a miracle."

With short rests Mary and Joseph traveled until noon. They had been wondering where they would eat their mid-day meal when they saw, not far from the road a beautiful little stream, cool and shady. Mary was delighted. Joseph lifted her down, and she ran to the stream and sat down beside it.

"It's beautiful Joseph," she said. "Almost like the stream near our house where we keep the milk and butter.

"And," she added thoughtfully, "where I conceived the child."

Joseph brought the lunch, and they spread it out on the ground. The donkeys were watered after Joseph had gotten a supply of water for Mary and himself, and they ate and enjoyed their food. After lunch Joseph sat leaning against a tree and Mary leaned against his broad shoulder and slept. They rested here for two hours and felt refreshed and happy to resume their journey.

And so Mary and Joseph traveled for several days on their way to Jerusalem to see Elizabeth. They had both made the journey many times to attend the feasts, but the sight of Jerusalem always quickened their pulses, and Mary was very excited as they neared the city's gates. They passed through the gates and became part of the teeming mass of travelers, merchants, and citizens of that great city. It took them some time to get across the city to where Elizabeth and Zachariah lived, but at last, just as the last rays of the sun made the sky seem a great fire, they arrived in the courtyard. The clatter of the two donkeys' hooves brought the running feet of two servants, and Elizabeth, sitting in the coolness on the other side of the courtyard, heard Mary's voice as she asked for Elizabeth.

Joseph never forgot this moment. Elizabeth, large with child in her sixth month, came clumsily to meet them, and Mary, having already alighted from the donkey, went running to meet her. The older woman clasped Mary in her arms, and, with tears running down her cheeks, said, * "Blessed are thou among women, and blessed is the fruit of thy womb. And whence is this to me, that the mother of my Lord should come to me? For, lo, as soon as the voice of thy saluation sounded in mine ears, the babe leaped in my womb for joy. And blessed is she that believed, for there shall be a performance of those things which were told her from the Lord."

Mary's words to Elizabeth were low and quiet, and Joseph could not hear what she said. He found that he had backed away from both of them as though afraid of treading on holy ground, and it was not until Mary turned, and with hand outstretched, beckoned him to her, that he went near them. With pride he told Elizabeth of their marriage, and Elizabeth kissed Joseph on the cheek in salutation.

"Welcome, Joseph," she said. "You are greatly honored to be the husband of the mother of our Lord. This great and wonderful thing that has happened to our people will overcome us all. We have waited long and patiently for our Messiah.

"But come, I know you are both weary from your journey. I will bring water for your feet and refreshment for your

*Luke 1:42–45

48

hunger." And Elizabeth called to her servant and led the way into a cool and comfortable room opening on the courtyard.

Mary and Joseph sank gratefully on the low couches, and when the servant brought the water and towels for their feet and washed them tenderly, Mary said, "I did not know I could get so tired riding. Poor Joseph, you must indeed be weary, having walked so far."

"I am weary, Mary," he answered, smiling at her, "but I shall recover quickly with food and drink."

The servant had withdrawn but returned in a few minutes with wine for Joseph and milk for Mary. There were figs and grapes on a platter also, and Elizabeth watched the two as they partook of the food with relish.

"Mary, Mary," she said. "You look so young and beautiful. And so happy that a light almost seems to surround you. Tell me of your experience with the Angel Gabriel? I know nothing of what has happened except the brief message from your father, which preceded you by only one day. You were almost as swift as the caravan courier."

Mary told her softly and with great emotion. She left out no detail. She even told of her father's and mother's unbelief and of Joseph's vision, of their marriage, and that of her sister.

Through it all, Elizabeth sat quietly and when Mary had finished, she said, "And my child, John, shall be the bearer of the good tidings that your son, Jesus, is the long-awaited Messiah." And she broke into tears and covered her face with her hands.

Joseph arose and left the two women alone. He walked out into the courtyard and finally into the street. He was fascinated by noise and confusion of the city after the quiet country life of Nazareth. He walked for a long time, watching the people walking, riding on donkeys, trading their wares until suddenly he realized he had arrived at the Temple. He thought about trying to find Elizabeth's husband, Zachariah, but he

knew that the priest would be busy with his duties and remembered that since the Angel had appeared unto him, he had been unable to speak. So, still thinking about the miracle, he turned and walked slowly back to the house of Elizabeth.

When he arrived in the courtyard, he was told by one of the servants that Mary was lying down in their room and Joseph followed him there. As he lifted the curtain that covered the doorway, he could see that she had removed her traveling clothes and had donned a loose-fitting house garment. She lay, asleep, with one hand tucked under her cheek and Joseph thought, tenderly, how much like a little girl she looked.

"I must be strong," he said aloud to himself. "You have much to go through. I do not understand it, my wife, as you seem to, but I shall try. No one shall harm you while I am near."

Outside, in the court, Joseph could hear Elizabeth's strong voice giving orders for their evening meal and he heard her step, slow and heavy, as she went to her room to rest. He felt suddenly very weary himself and lay down on a couch near Mary's where he could watch her sweet face, but soon his eyes closed and he slept also, a deep and dreamless sleep, and did not awaken until he felt the gentle touch of Mary's hand on his face.

"It is night, my husband," she said softly. "Elizabeth has prepared our evening meal and Zachariah has come to greet us."

Joseph nodded, smiled into her eyes, and arose. She went quietly out into the court, and he could hear her laughter now and then. After bathing his face, Joseph went out also and saw that Zachariah was listening to Mary in rapt attention. Suddenly, however, he saw Joseph and arose with outstretched hands. Joseph went to him quickly, and, clasping Zachariah's hands in his, touched both cheeks with his lips in the Jewish salutation.

"I'm glad to see you, Zachariah," Joseph said. "And the

hospitality you and Elizabeth offer Mary and me is most appreciated."

Zachariah nodded his head gravely and smiled. Sitting back down he motioned Joseph into a seat nearby and, nodding at Mary, motioned her to continue.

She told again of her wonderful experience. Then suddenly she grew sorrowful and sad. "My father, Zachariah, has made me promise I will tell no one of my experience except you and Elizabeth. He feels that the people in Nazareth should think my baby is the son of my husband. How will our people know he is the Messiah if I keep all these things a secret?"

Zachariah arose and went into the house, and Mary was left with a look of wonder on her face at his abruptness. Elizabeth said, quickly, "He has gone to write an answer for you. He will return in a few moments. He comes home very seldom since the appearance of the Angel and spends most of his time praying and attending to his duties in the Temple. I sent one of the servants to tell him you had come, and he came at once to see you."

In a few moments, Zachariah returned, and a servant, holding a light, came with him. He handed Mary a writing tablet on which were written these words: "Your father is right. You would be laughed to scorn and perhaps persecuted by our enemies. Guard your secret well and God in his time will reveal the Messiah in His own way. I did not trust Him and was struck dumb for my unbelief. The son Elizabeth and I are to have will be a great prophet and we need have no fear that God will see that the world knows the Messiah has come. Speak to no one of what you have seen or heard and let the people think the child belongs to Joseph. It is the safest thing for all of us."

Mary looked up, after reading the tablet, and nodded in agreement. She handed it to Joseph and then to Elizabeth, and the four sat in silence, thinking, until a servant announced their evening meal.

After they had all eaten heartily, Zachariah returned to the Temple, with the promise that he would return the first chance he had to see them again. He had written also that he was glad Mary was to be with Elizabeth. He clasped Joseph's hands in his, and a mutual understanding seemed to pass between them. "I shall stay close by," Joseph said. "You need have no fear for either of them."

They retired early but Mary and Joseph talked long into the night about how long they would stay with Elizabeth and what Joseph could do while there.

"I think," Mary said "that I shall stay until John is born. It is but three months, and perhaps you could find work here to take up your time if you get tired watching over Elizabeth and me."

"We shall see," Joseph answered. "And I think to stay with Elizabeth until after her son comes is good, but we must get back to Nazareth soon after that for your sake."

Mary smiled sleepily and fondly at him and thought how good and kind a man he was. She felt warm and comforted that he was near, and when he lay down beside her for the night, she snuggled into his strong arms with a sigh. He kissed her tenderly, and as she went to sleep, he let his mind play a little on the day when she would have delievered her son and would be his wife in every way.

IV

The days passed quickly for Mary as she and Elizabeth awaited the birth of Elizabeth's son. They spent many long hours sitting in the warm sunshine of the courtyard, talking about their unborn children and the mission of both in the world. Elizabeth, more wise in religious matters than Mary, tried to help her understand the prophecies and what the Jewish race expected in the Savior that was to come.

Mary listened carefully but admitted she really comprehended but little. She was still awed as to why it should have been she who was chosen, and in her simple faith prayed constantly that she would be able to carry out her part of the miracle, but down in her heart, she knew she did not understand it at all. She understood the coming of Elizabeth's son much better than she did her own, as she had been reared on stories of the great prophets of her race.

Joseph, though an intelligent man, was slow thinking and as a rule very practical. He had been educated in the Jewish religion, as most men of his class were, but he understood even less than Mary the coming of a Savior. He, like his wife, just accepted the fact that she was to bear the Son of God and tried not to think further than that on the subject. He spent his time doing small carpentry jobs about the neighborhood of Elizabeth's home and kept himself so busy that he did not have to time to think about all the weighty problems that might be ahead.

Zachariah had found him almost more work than he could do, and he seldom noticed the passing of time, until the night Mary awakened him hurriedly, saying that Elizabeth's child was being born and he was to go in all haste for Zachariah, who was at the Temple.

Mary, who had led a most sheltered life with Anna and Heli, had never been around a woman in labor and as she stood by Elizabeth, holding her hand, she was pale and shaky. Elizabeth, being old, was experiencing great agony, and there were times before the child was born when Mary thought she had died.

Several neighbor women had come in, as the two servants had been dispatched quietly to arouse them, and Mary also felt somewhat better when she heard the voices of Joseph and Zachariah in the courtyard.

Zachariah looked pale and worried in the flickering light of the torches, and Mary hastened to reassure him of Elizabeth's condition, even though she did not feel the confidence she portrayed.

"She is in good hands, Zachariah, and you must not worry."

He nodded his head and sat down with Joseph to await the child.

Mary, going back to Elizabeth, was appalled at the horrible pain she was suffering, and as the minutes grew to hours, she feared for Elizabeth's life even more. Finally, however, toward dawn the child was born, and he was laid in Elizabeth's arms for a moment before she went into a deep sleep.

Mary, exhausted after the long night of waiting on her cousin and weak from the emotional and mental strain, slept fitfully for several hours after the sun came up. In her dreams it was she who was having the baby, and once Joseph gently awakened her when she screamed out in pain. Joseph thought, as he watched her go back to sleep, how very young she was and that the ordeal she had seen Elizabeth go through was much more of a shock than he had realized.

However, after she had awakened, she seemed refreshed

and once more calm and serene. When she went in to see about Elizabeth, she was smiling with pleasure, and Elizabeth, seeing her come through the doorway, smiled in response, and tears of joy streamed down her face.

"My son, Mary, bring him to me." Though she was weak, her voice was natural and eager.

And, Mary, laying the child in her arms, said, "Elizabeth, he is a fine child and very beautiful. Zachariah is so pleased he cannot return to the Temple. He has started back three or four times, but always is delayed by a neighbor visiting, and though he cannot speak, his eyes talk. And he has written on the tablet so much about his son that Joseph is beginning to tease him. I think he now wishes to see you and the child once more before he goes."

As Zachariah came into the bedchamber, Mary left and found Joseph sitting in the courtyard staring into the morning sky. She put her hand lightly on his shoulder. He reached up and, taking her fingers in his, said "We must now return to Nazareth, Mary. I have left your father long enough with all the work."

"Yes, Joseph, it is time we returned," Mary replied. "Elizabeth asks that we stay for the circumcision, and I have told her it would have to be your decision as I knew you were most anxious to return home."

"I have told Zachariah we would remain until the circumcision, but would have to leave the next day," he answered. "I do not want you to delay traveling any longer than is absolutely necessary."

Mary did not say anything for a few minutes, then she said quietly, "Joseph, Zachariah says that the Son of God is to be born in Bethlehem, according to the prophecies."

Joseph looked at Mary in amazement. "Bethlehem? But surely, Mary, he is mistaken. We live in Nazareth, and there your child will be born. We cannot go to Bethlehem. We have no home there, and my place is with your father."

Mary, seeing Joseph's concern, spoke gently. "Yes, Joseph. I did not mean that we should go to Bethlehem now. I only wondered about the prophecy. The Angel Gabriel, did not tell me where the child was to be born, only that he was to be of the House of David." And, she added proudly, "I am of the House of David. We both are, being kinsmen. Your father and mine came from Bethlehem. But I shall not worry about it, and we shall return home the day following the circumcision of the child."

Joseph, relieved, watched Mary go back to Elizabeth with a smile.

Elizabeth's strength did not return after her baby's birth, and she found she could not stay up but an hour or so at a time. She wanted Mary with her all the time and would have begged her to remain until after the birth of her child had she not known how anxious Joseph was to return home. She dreaded to see Mary leave and felt that her own days were numbered. However, when the day for the circumcision arrived, she steeled herself against fatigue and arose very early to get her household in readiness for the neighbors and cousins who would come in for the sacred rites performed by the Hebrew people on the eighth day of a male child's life. This ceremony, performed by the priest, celebrated the covenant between God and Abraham, and on this day, also, they would name the child.

Elizabeth, with the help of Mary, had gotten all in readiness, and when her guests arrived, they rejoiced with Elizabeth that she was now the mother of a son. The priest and others from the Temple arrived with Zachariah, and after the child was circumcised, the priest called him "Zachariah," after his father and laid the child in Elizabeth's arms.

The entire company was startled, however, when she said quietly, "His name is John."

They all turned to her and several of her cousins said, "But, Elizabeth, there is no one of thy kindred named John. What does Zachariah say to all this?"

And, Zachariah, smiling, picked up his writing tablet and wrote on it, "His name is John."

He then took his son into his arms and there came over him a look of exultation. For the first time in over nine months, his voice sounded over the room, deep and resonant, and he said, * "Blessed be the Lord God of Israel, for he hath visited and redeemed his people, and hath raised up a horn of salvation for us in the house of his servant David, as he spake by the mouth of his holy prophets, which have been since the world began; that we should be saved from our enemies, and from the hand of all that hate us, to perform the mercy promised to our fathers, and to remember his holy covenant, the oath which he sware to our father Abraham, that he would grant unto us, that we, being delivered out of the hand of our enemies, might serve him without fear, in holiness and righteousness before him, all the days of our life. And thou, child, shall be called the prophet of the Highest, for thou shalt go before the face of the Lord to prepare his ways; to give knowledge of salvation unto his people by the remission of their sins, through the tender mercy of our God, whereby the dayspring from on high hath visited us, to give light to them that sit in darkness and in the shadow of death, to guide our feet into the way of peace."

Every face had turned to Zachariah when he began to speak, and at the end of his words, there was silence. No one who had heard his words would ever forget them, and they looked with awe at Zachariah and the tiny baby held in his arms. They turned silently away from him, then began to murmur among themselves. Only when they were partaking of the feast

*Luke 1:67–79

58

prepared for them, and as they sat on the divans around the room where the feast was served, they talked in awed whispers about the child. Some were frightened and left the house as soon as it was proper, while others, fascinated by Zachariah's sudden speech, stayed to talk with him and Elizabeth and to look anew at the baby.

And it was not until the next day that Elizabeth and Zachariah found how widely spread the talk had become, for suddenly they became very popular, and strangers would come and talk with Zachariah for hours about the child and men from the Temple questioned him closely, but something warned him not to talk too much and he was very glad that Mary and Joseph had left.

For they did leave the day after the celebration, and Mary found on her journey home that she did not feel as well as she thought she had. When at last she saw her mother's face, smiling and full of love, she realized how glad she was to be back home safely.

And Zachariah, in Jerusalem, made plans quietly with Elizabeth to leave and take their small son to distant relatives and live out the remainder of their days teaching John the laws of Moses and preparing him for the great work they knew he would perform.

*   *   *

Night was under a myriad of stars, and Mary and Joseph were silent as they looked into the clear beauty of the sky. The wind was sharp and cool, and Mary pulled her cloak around her tightly and let out a little sigh. Joseph, upon hearing it, turned quickly and asked, "Are you all right my wife? We will be in Bethlehem soon now."

Mary smiled her serene smile, tender and sweet, at her

husband. "Yes, Joseph, I'm all right—don't have concern for me."

Joseph looked at Mary in the awed manner he sometimes had when he heard her speak, so softly, yet with so much confidence and no fear. He thought about how angry Heli and Anna, even he, had been, when Mary had insisted on accompanying him to Bethlehem to pay the taxes that Caesar had decreed was to be done in the country in which a man had been born. Heli, also born in Bethlehem, had been exempt when Joseph had promised to pay his tax for him, and it was not necessary that Mary go. But, quietly, and with none of the usual submissiveness, so much a part of the Jewish woman, Mary had stated she was going to Bethlehem and no argument on the part of her parents or Joseph would change her. She had finally convinced Joseph that she had to go, and he had given in. She was quite concerned for him because he had worried so—but when she and he had arrived in Jerusalem safely, he had breathed a sigh of relief and had relaxed a little. They had refreshed themselves with food and rest and now they were almost in Bethlehem, after the five-mile journey from the city.

Joseph, in deep thought, walked along, his mind on paying the taxes and finding a place for Mary to sleep. He had heard in Jerusalem that the tiny little town of Bethlehem was very crowded and that he would have difficulty finding a room, but again, Mary had been absolutely determined to go on that night. Her very insistence had made such an impression on Joseph that he gave up without argument again, his plan that they stay in Jerusalem until morning.

All of a sudden, on the rise of a small hill, Mary and Joseph looked down on Bethlehem. Flares from torches gleamed like tiny stars and the hills all around the town shone in the starry night like jewels set around a diamond.

"Joseph," Mary said, "have you ever seen the stars as they are tonight? They are so brilliant." Then she stopped suddenly.

For as she spoke, the stars seemed to fade from the sky, one at a time, but quickly, and all the sky became a rich, velvet darkness.

Joseph was stunned, and frightened. Mary felt a queer feeling of awe take hold of her, but she was not afraid. She seemed to understand something that Joseph did not. She whispered a word of comfort to him and spoke quietly, "Let us go quickly, Joseph. My time is at hand."

Her husband turned to look at her in horror. "But, Mary, we have no place yet. What shall I do?"

"Just let us get to the inn, Joseph. There we will find a place."

Joseph touched the donkey's side, and he and the animal quickened their pace. Mary strained her eyes to the sky. No star was now visible and only the moon shone in all its glory.

As Mary and Joseph came up to the inn, they could hear the noise of the crowd in the courtyard. Men sat around small fires, camels and donkeys cluttered up every available spot, and soldiers roamed around looking at the crowd, their rough laughter and conversation with one another being heard over the quiet speech of the Jews there for the purpose of paying taxes.

The innkeeper listened to Joseph's request for a room in silence. He, however, when he heard Joseph's story about Mary, looked sympathetically at him and said, "My good friend, there is no room, no room at all. We are so crowded that many of the people are sleeping in the courtyard, as you can see."

Joseph's stricken face made the landlord almost angry in his inability to help him. Then he caught sight of Mary on the donkey. Her beautiful dark eyes searched him for help, and he turned away and called to his wife. "Come, see if you can help this man and his wife." And he left the doorway as a woman about fifty years of age came to the door.

She looked at Mary in astonishment. "Woman," she said, "why are you here?"

Mary, still serene and beautiful, merely nodded her head and smiled as Joseph said in a hoarse voice, "Quickly, can we find a warm place for my wife? She is about to be delievered of her first child."

The woman stood for a moment, then said, "The only place she can go is the stable. It is warm there and far enough from this crowd for privacy. Come, I will show you."

Joseph, grateful, took the donkey by the bridle and led him as the woman hurriedly showed them the way to the stable.

She had picked up a torch, which had been hanging by the door, and she handed it to Joseph as they reached the stable. She said, "I'll come back when I get a chance, and bring you something to eat and drink. She will be all right here," she added, as Joseph looked about the stable. "It is clean and warm, and women have babies every day, sir, and are all right."

Mary whispered her thanks as the woman left, but before she had taken a step, she suddenly turned and looked at Mary. Something about Mary's face there in the light of the torch made the woman stare in awed silence for a moment. Then, shaking her head, she left.

Joseph put away the donkey where he could eat and the little bells tinkled softly as he moved his head. The sheep lay sleeping and a lamb would cry occasionally like a small baby. The camels stood or knelt about outside, patiently chewing or looking wise.

Joseph moved about in the stable quietly, watching with anxious eyes as Mary prepared herself for the night on the straw bed. She covered it with her cloak, and Joseph handed her his to use as a cover. Suddenly she straightened up and looked at him, and her eyes widened. Joseph thought about that look later many times. It was the look of thousands of women about to give birth to their firstborn child, except from her eyes was missing fear. There was no fear, only concern that he would be disturbed and worried about her.

"Joseph," she said, "my child is about to be born."

"Mary," was all he could say. His voice choked and sweat seemed to pour from every pore in his body. His hands suddenly shook and he could not move.

Mary watched him a moment, then in a quiet voice went on, "Joseph, go into the inn and see if the innkeeper's wife can come back. Go, Joseph, don't just stand there and stare at me. I haven't long to wait and I will need her with me."

Then she added softly, with a strange tone to her voice, "Remember, Joseph, 'tis no ordinary child I am bearing. Know you not that God will deliver me safely?"

Joseph visibly relaxed, and going to Mary, he kissed her on the forehead and hastily left for the inn.

Mary, in the meantime, knelt in the straw and prepared her bed and herself the best she knew how for the birth of her son.

In a few minutes, the innkeeper's wife arrived at the stable. Looking at Mary, she said, "Your husband tells me you are about to be delivered of your first child."

"Yes," Mary answered quietly. "I am, and I would like for you to be with me. My husband is so anxious and frightened for me that he is not of much help."

"Are you not frightened, my child?" the woman asked. "You look in no pain, and I am not sure you are about to be delievered."

"I am sure," Mary said, "very sure, and there will be no pain."

The woman started to say something, then changed her mind and said instead, "My name is Ruth, child. What is yours and your husband's?"

"My name is Mary," came the answer, "and my husband's

name is Joseph. We are of the House of David and have come to be taxed."

Outside Joseph could hear the women's voices as they spoke low, and although he could not catch their words, their tones indicated they were becoming friends and he was glad the woman had come out to be with Mary.

Suddenly the stable was very quiet. No sound came out to him, no animal made a sound, and the whole world seemed to become silent. And in the silence, right above the stable, a huge and brilliant star suddenly appeared directly over the stable. Its beams seemed to reach in all directions, and Joseph's eyes could not leave it. It was the only star in the sky, and he had never seen anything like it. Its beauty was beyond anything he had had ever seen, and as suddenly as it had appeared, he realized what it meant. The child had been born, and he moved slowly toward the stable door as Ruth came out.

"You have a son," she said softly, "a beautiful son, and your wife is calling for you. Tell me, sir, before you go in to her, what kind of woman is she, and the child, why is he so beautiful and just born? She suffered no pain at all and does not seem to even know she has had a child."

Joseph only shook his head and looked up at the star, and the woman, looking with him gasped in astonishment. Joseph left her abruptly, with a word of thanks and a pressure to her hand, to go into Mary.

"This is a strange night," the woman murmured to herself, "a strange night. Something great and wonderful has happened here, but perhaps I had better keep silent." And she returned to the inn.

Joseph knelt by Mary and the tiny beautiful child she held in her arms and kissed her softly, then looked at the baby in wonder.

"He is so beautiful, Joseph, is he not? And so tiny. And,

the Son of God, Joseph, the Son of God. How can we be worthy of Him, this tiny child of God?"

Joseph could not speak. He kissed the baby's tiny fingers and touched the soft little cheek with his big fingers. "The Son of God; and, Mary, you should see the star his Father sent to hail his birth. It is shining over the stable in all the brilliance of all the stars put together."

Joseph watched Mary for a long time, and finally she slept with the baby close to her. He slept also.

Toward morning Joseph heard a noise and realized that several people were outside the stable door. He could hear the voice of Ruth as she tried to make them leave. Then one voice said loudly, "But we want to see the babe. We know he was born here last night. We have seen the star and signs from Heaven, music from choirs of angels, and we have come to worship him."

Ruth was astounded. "There was a child born here last night, but what you say is foolish." Then she stopped. "No, you may be right. Come see the babe. I will go also."

Then, Joseph, having arisen from the straw, saw a strange group of shepherds enter the stable, their staffs in their hands and faces eager and expectant. "We have come; they said, "to see the Son of God."

They approached Mary reverently and softly. Mary, who had awakened, watched the shepherds as they knelt to look at the sleeping child she held in her arms.

"Is it true?" one asked. "Is it true that he is the Son of God?"

Mary, nodding her head, held the baby where they could see him. "But," she added softly, "tell no one, for there are those about who would harm him," and they nodded in silence.

They left after a time, and Ruth brought Mary and Joseph something to eat.

Mary held her baby in her arms tenderly and looked at

Joseph with love. When she spoke, it was with an awed and wonderful voice. Finally she said, "Joseph, it is true. He is the Son of God and he is here. Now let us go home and await God's Word for his life." Joseph nodded and watched her in loving tenderness.

Joseph talked all through the day to shepherds and strangers who came quietly and secretly to look and kneel before the babe Mary held in her arms or who lay in the manger peacefully sleeping.

And, Mary, quiet and thoughtfully, listened and pondered all these things in her heart.